The Very Sleepy Sloth

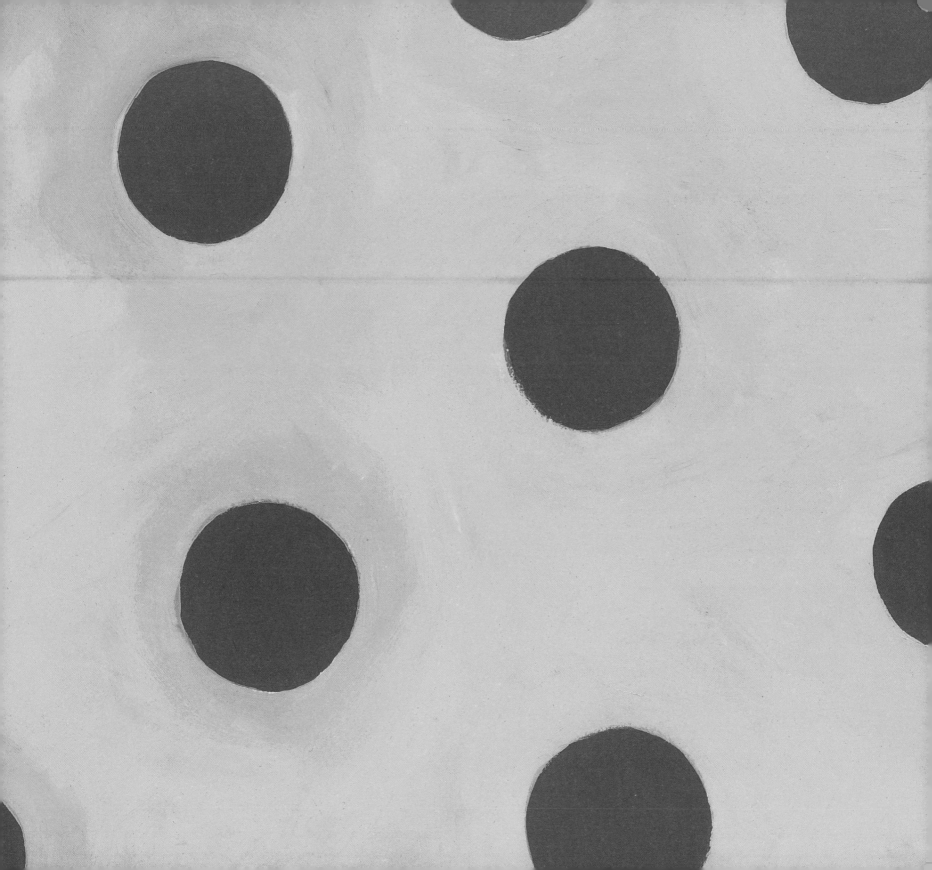

For Joyce, Ashifa and everyone
at Ottakar's Bromley
—A.M.

For Jazz
—J.T.

ISBN 0-439-68068-9

Text copyright © 2003 by Andrew Murray. Illustrations copyright
© 2003 by Jack Tickle. All rights reserved. Published by Scholastic Inc.,
557 Broadway, New York, NY 10012, by arrangement with Tiger Tales,
an imprint of ME Media LLC. SCHOLASTIC and associated logos are
trademarks and/or registered trademarks of Scholastic Inc.

12 11 10 9 8 7 6 5 4 3 2 1   4 5 6 7 8 9/0

Printed in the U.S.A.   40

First Scholastic printing, October 2004

The Very Sleepy Sloth

by
Andrew Murray

illustrated by
Jack Tickle

SCHOLASTIC INC.

New York   Toronto   London   Auckland   Sydney
Mexico City   New Delhi   Hong Kong   Buenos Aires

Early one morning, deep
in the jungle, Sloth was
fast asleep.
    But the rest of the
animals were wide awake.

Cheetah was on the treadmill, working on his

SPEED.

Elephant was lifting heavy weights, working on her

STRENGTH.

Kangaroo was
on the trampoline,
working on her

SPRING.

Monkey was
on the high bars,
working on his

SWING.

While Sloth stayed in his hammock, working on his sleep.

"That Sloth is so lazy," said Cheetah.

"All he does is lie there!" agreed Elephant.

"Just dozing in his hammock," added Kangaroo.

"Hey, Sloth!" called Monkey. "We're all working hard here. Why don't you get up and do something?"

Sloth slowly opened one eye. "Monkey," he said. "If you're so hard-working, you try lifting Elephant's weights."

"Easy!" said Monkey, and
he tried to lift the weights.
Elephant giggled as...

oooooooof!

Monkey toppled right over.

"Elephant!" said Monkey gruffly. "If you think it's so easy, you jump like Kangaroo!"

So Elephant tried to
jump on the trampoline.
Kangaroo shook her
head as . . .

CRASH!

Elephant fell right through. "Don't look at me like that, Kangaroo!" said Elephant grumpily. "Can you run like Cheetah?"

So Kangaroo tried the treadmill.

Cheetah chuckled as Kangaroo landed . . .

on her bottom!

OOOOOOW!

"Cheetah!" said Kangaroo angrily. "If you're so smart, you swing like Monkey."

So Cheetah climbed
the high bars and
swung right into...

Elephant.

EEE E EK!

By now, everyone was very hot,
very tired, and very, very cranky.
"This is useless," they muttered.
"Who caused all this trouble?"

"It wasn't me," said Elephant.
"I was busy lifting weights."

"And it wasn't me," said Monkey.
"I was busy swinging."
All the animals turned and
looked at . . .

SLOTH!

"Hey Sloth," they called.
"You started all this!"

Sloth turned lazily. "You must see by now," he said. "We were all busy doing what we do best. Even me!"

The animals thought about it. "Yes!" they cried. "We're all good at running or jumping or lifting or swinging. But Sloth is the very best at . . ."

"SNO

OZING!"

"Exactly!" said Sloth.
And with a stretch and a
yawn he fell fast asleep!